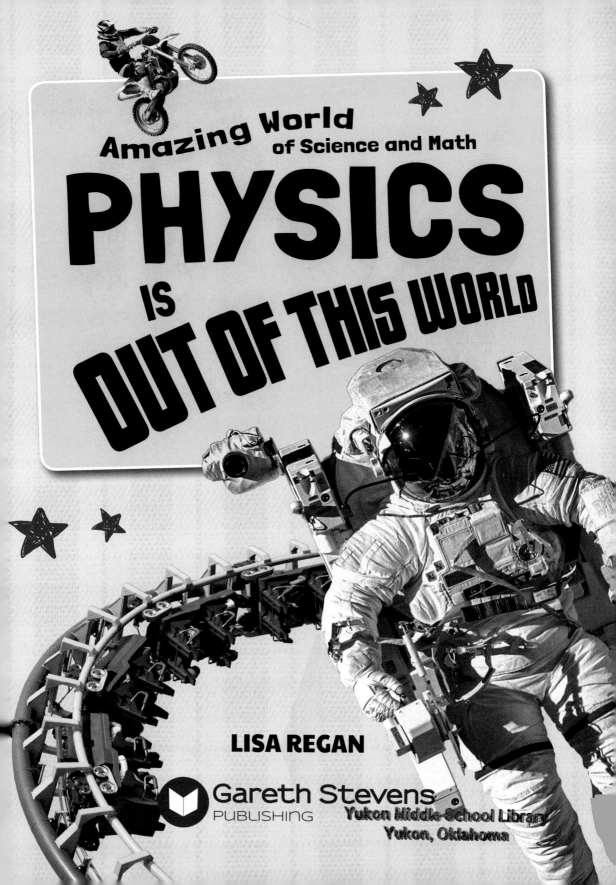

Amazing World of Science and Math

PHYSICS IS OUT OF THIS WORLD

LISA REGAN

Gareth Stevens
PUBLISHING

Please visit our website, www.garethstevens.com.
For a free color catalog of all our high-quality books,
call toll free 1-800-542-2595 or fax 1-877-542-2596.

Cataloging-in-Publication Data

Names: Regan, Lisa.
Title: Physics is out of this world / Lisa Regan.
Description: New York : Gareth Stevens Publishing, 2017. | Series: Amazing world of science
    and math | Includes index.
Identifiers: ISBN 9781482449822 (pbk.) | ISBN 9781482449846 (library bound) |
    ISBN 9781482449839 (6 pack)
Subjects: LCSH: Physics–Juvenile literature.
Classification: LCC QC25.R44 2017 | DDC 530–dc23

Published in 2017 by
Gareth Stevens Publishing
111 East 14ᵗʰ Street, Suite 349
New York, NY 10003

All images from Shutterstock except p6 NASA; p12 Byelikova Oksana / Shutterstock.com;
p37(b) homydesign / Shutterstock.com; p39(t) Rainer Herhaus / Shutterstock.com; p40 Nasa /
Shutterstock; p41(b) Nasa.

Printed in the United States of America
CPSIA compliance information: Batch CS16GS:
For further information contact Gareth Stevens, New York, New York at 1-800-542-2595.

Contents

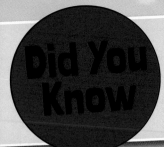

LIGHT IS 18 MILLION TIMES FASTER THAN RAIN

Light travels through space at a constant speed. It is the fastest thing there is. Rain travels at varying speeds, but it's certainly a lot, lot slower than light!

Space travel

In the **vacuum** of space, where there are virtually no atoms to slow it down, light travels 186,000 miles in a second. It takes about eight minutes for the sun's light to reach us here on Earth. Astronomers (scientists who study space) use the speed of light to measure vast distances in the universe. A light-year is the distance that light can travel in one year. Our galaxy, the Milky Way, is about 150,000 light-years across.

LIGHT CAN TRAVEL AROUND THE EARTH SEVEN TIMES IN ONE SECOND.

On the move

Light is a form of energy that travels in waves. It moves in a straight line, which is why you cannot see around a corner! It can pass through some things, such as air or water, but the particles in those things slow it down. It can also pass through transparent objects, such as glass. It cannot pass through some things, such as bricks or trees. These items are said to be opaque.

Playing with light

There are three main ways to control light. It can be blocked by objects, forming a shadow. It can also be bounced back, or reflected (see page 7) and bent, or **refracted** (see page 8).

TRANSLUCENT MATERIALS ALLOW SOME LIGHT TO PASS THROUGH, BUT NOT ENOUGH TO SEE THROUGH IT CLEARLY.

Hot and cold

Light energy often goes hand in hand with heat energy. A light bulb gets hotter as it gives off light. A burning candle emits both light and heat energy together. Hot light is called **incandescence**. However, not all light sources give off heat. Cold light is called **luminescence**, and is found in nature. Fireflies and many deep sea creatures create their own cold light by mixing different chemicals in their body. This is the same kind of light as a party glow stick. When you snap the stick, you allow the chemicals to mix together and cause a reaction that gives off light energy.

THE HUBBLE TELESCOPE CAN'T LOOK AT THE SUN

The Hubble Space Telescope (HST) was the first telescope to view space from above Earth's atmosphere. It can see galaxies that are trillions of miles away, but it cannot focus on the sun without frying its delicate equipment.

High in the sky

The HST is not a telescope that you look through with your eye pressed up to it. It uses a digital camera to take photos, and beams them back to be studied in detail. Before its invention, telescopes were pointed into space from Earth's surface. They have to look through the atmosphere, which changes and blocks some of the light. Hubble orbits above the atmosphere, so it can see more clearly.

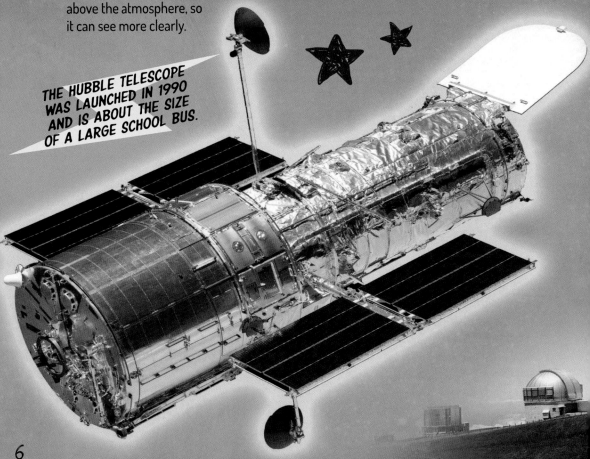

THE HUBBLE TELESCOPE WAS LAUNCHED IN 1990 AND IS ABOUT THE SIZE OF A LARGE SCHOOL BUS.

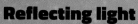
I'm seeing stars!

Isaac Newton
(1642–1727)

Reflecting light

Light travels in straight lines (see page 5) and bounces off objects that get in its way. If the object is smooth and shiny, like a mirror or a smooth lake, the light reflects back to produce a clear image. If the object is irregular, like windblown water, the light is reflected in several directions and the image gets disrupted.

Banish the blur

The earliest telescopes used for looking at the stars produced blurry images. In the 1680s Isaac Newton invented a new kind of telescope with mirrors inside, which gave a much clearer view of the night skies. Called a reflecting telescope, it has a curved mirror which collects light from a distant object and reflects it so it becomes focused, or clearer to see. Another mirror reflects this focused image out of the telescope through an eyepiece.

A clearer view

Many telescopes are placed in a dome-shaped building called an observatory. They are often built on mountaintops, where the air is thinner and the view is clearer. There are 13 different telescopes on top of Mauna Kea, a dormant volcano in Hawaii. The island's position near the equator, in the middle of the Pacific Ocean where the skies are dark, dry, and cloud-free, makes it a prime spot for looking far into space.

THE MAUNA KEA OBSERVATORY IS HOME TO THREE OF THE WORLD'S LARGEST TELESCOPES.

A rainbow is a spectacular light show that happens when sunlight and water droplets occur together. You will only see it if you are standing with the sun behind you.

Dividing light

Sunlight is known as white light, but is made up of different shades combined together. A rainbow forms when light hits a raindrop and is refracted, or bent. The light rays slow down as they pass from air into water, and travel at different speeds. They reflect off the inside of the raindrop, and bounce back out at different angles. This forms the curved rainbow, with red at the top and violet at the bottom.

Rainbows—not just for rainy days.

Make a rainbow

White light can be split into its **spectrum** of shades using a **prism**. A prism is a triangular glass block that refracts light as it passes through. The light is separated according to its wavelengths. Red has the longest wavelength and so is refracted the least. You may notice the rainbow effect happening in other situations: a fountain, waterfall, or the spray from a hose can perform the same feat. If you view a rainbow from the air, such as from a plane, it can form a full circle.

Beyond the visible

There are some rays which the human eye cannot see. Infrared and microwaves have longer wavelengths, and radio waves have the longest wavelength of them all. Microwaves can be used for cooking, but also for carrying signals for phones. **Ultraviolet** (UV) light has a shorter wavelength than the violet part of the spectrum. It can cause sunburn and make things glow. The shortest wavelengths are X-rays and gamma rays, used in medicine for detecting broken bones or cancer.

Did You Know

Sunlight can be reflected twice inside a raindrop, forming a double rainbow.

Hidden from view

Humans can't see UV light, but some creatures can. Scientists have found that bees can see UV markings on flowers that guide them straight to the nectar supplies. Reindeer rely on UV light for finding lichens to eat. Some birds use UV patterns to distinguish males from females. It's a whole world that is invisible to humans!

Did You Know

YOUR EYES SEE UPSIDE DOWN

Light bounces off objects and into your eyes, where the image is passed to your brain to make sense of the world. But the image formed in your eye is flipped on its head!

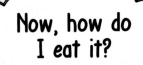

Now, how do I eat it?

THE LENS IN YOUR EYE CHANGES SHAPE TO FOCUS SO THAT YOU DON'T SEE BLURRED IMAGES.

Seeing the light

Light enters your eye through a section at the front, like a window, called the cornea. It passes through a curved lens that bends the light rays to focus them, and creates an upside-down image on the surface at the back of the eye. This surface is called the retina, and its function is to turn light into signals that your brain can understand. The brain very cleverly flips the upside-down messages so that you see the world the right way up.

Darkness and light

The retina has different types of cells to perform different jobs. It contains around 7 million cones, which are sensitive to red, green, or blue light. They work together to allow you to see millions of different shades. The retina also has rods, which see in black and white. They are sensitive to light and dark and allow you to see shapes and movement, even in very low light.

All in your mind

A strawberry is red, round, and you can feel its **mass** when you hold it, right? Well, kind of. It certainly has a definite mass and shape, but its "redness" is something you see, rather than a physical quality. Light hits an object and either bounces off or is absorbed, depending on its wavelength. A strawberry absorbs all the light except the wavelengths that look red when they hit the cones in your retina. If you were a dog or a fish, you wouldn't see it as red at all.

CATS AND DOGS CAN'T SEE THE DIFFERENCE BETWEEN RED AND GREEN.

Playing tricks

Sometimes your brain can be tricked into seeing things that aren't real. Your eye gathers information that your brain tries to interpret and turn into some kind of sense. Optical illusions play with your vision and your brain to make you see things that don't match reality.

Too much visual information tricks the brain into thinking shapes are moving.

THE LOUDEST SOUND EVER WAS A VOLCANO

When Mount Krakatoa erupted in 1883 the sound was heard 3,000 miles (4,800 km) away in Mauritius. It was the loudest sound in recorded history.

What a noise

A volcano erupts when gas bubbles force magma (molten rock) high into the air. It creates sound waves that travel far around Earth. All sounds are made when objects move or vibrate, making the air around them vibrate. The sounds travel as waves of energy that hit your eardrum. Your brain translates the vibrations in your eardrum into recognizable noises, whether it's a dog barking, a bell ringing, or a volcano exploding.

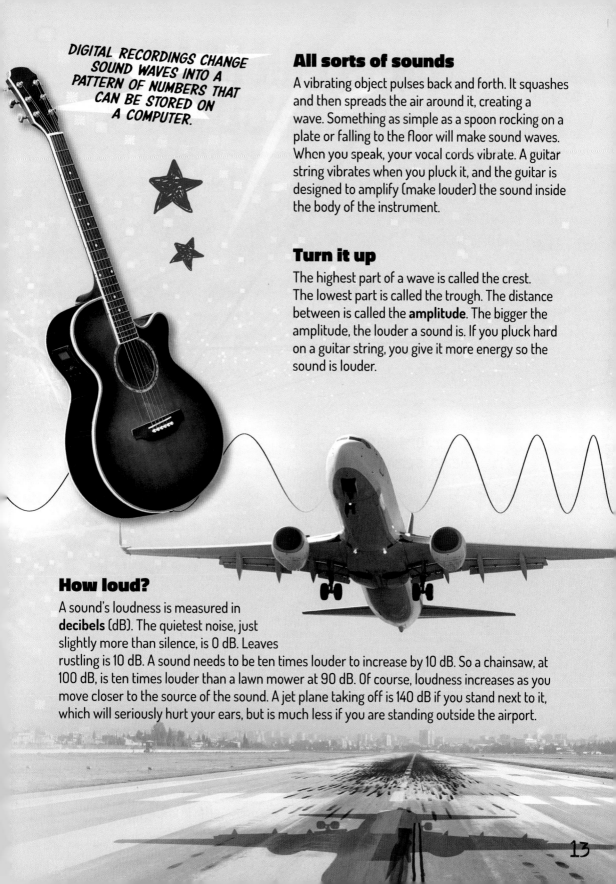

All sorts of sounds

A vibrating object pulses back and forth. It squashes and then spreads the air around it, creating a wave. Something as simple as a spoon rocking on a plate or falling to the floor will make sound waves. When you speak, your vocal cords vibrate. A guitar string vibrates when you pluck it, and the guitar is designed to amplify (make louder) the sound inside the body of the instrument.

Turn it up

The highest part of a wave is called the crest. The lowest part is called the trough. The distance between is called the **amplitude**. The bigger the amplitude, the louder a sound is. If you pluck hard on a guitar string, you give it more energy so the sound is louder.

How loud?

A sound's loudness is measured in **decibels** (dB). The quietest noise, just slightly more than silence, is 0 dB. Leaves rustling is 10 dB. A sound needs to be ten times louder to increase by 10 dB. So a chainsaw, at 100 dB, is ten times louder than a lawn mower at 90 dB. Of course, loudness increases as you move closer to the source of the sound. A jet plane taking off is 140 dB if you stand next to it, which will seriously hurt your ears, but is much less if you are standing outside the airport.

DOGS CAN HEAR THINGS YOU CAN'T

A dog's ears collect more sounds than yours, and from farther away. But they also hear noises that are outside the range of human hearing.

High-pitched hearing

Some sounds are high; others are low. That's because they have different pitches, or **frequencies**. Frequency measures the number of waves per second in a sound wave, and it is measured in **hertz** (Hz). A high-pitched noise has more waves per second; the waves are squeezed closer together. Humans can only hear higher-pitched noises between around 20 Hz and 20,000 Hz. Dogs can hear much higher-pitched noises: as much as 60,000 Hz.

I hear breakfast being served...

LOW-PITCHED NOISES, SUCH AS THUNDER, HAVE A LONG WAVELENGTH.

Pitch perfect

A piano can make notes of varying pitch. The keys on the left make low notes, and the pitch increases as you move to the right. The strings attached to the keys are different lengths and thicknesses.

Did You Know Sound travels more slowly than light. That's why you see lightning before you hear thunder.

Moving sound

The energy in a sound wave passes easily between air **molecules**. Sound has to have a medium to travel through, such as air, water, glass, or metal. It cannot travel through a vacuum where there are no particles to carry it.

Animal song

Sounds that are too high-pitched for people to hear are called **ultrasound**. They can be used in medicine, to look inside the body and check blood flow. Many creatures have ultrasonic hearing, not only dogs. Bats and dolphins can hear over 100,000 Hz and use echolocation to find their way around and capture prey. They send out high-pitched sounds and listen to the echoes that bounce back. Low-frequency sounds travel long distances through water. Some whales "sing" as low as 30 Hz to communicate over thousands of miles.

Whale song can travel through water for thousands of miles.

Different notes

A musical instrument's pitch depends on the size of the moving part, or how tightly it is stretched. A small drum makes a higher note than a big drum. A short string makes a higher note than a long string. Many instruments make a range of sounds. A guitar's strings are different thicknesses, and can be tightened or loosened to produce different notes.

Did You Know

Elephants can detect low sounds through their feet: as low as 5 Hz.

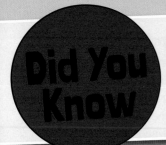

Did You Know

MARSHMALLOWS MELT AT MACH 1.6

Sound waves travel VERY quickly. Supersonic things move faster than the speed of sound, also known as Mach 1. That's fast enough to heat things up, making a marshmallow turn to goo.

What is the speed of sound?

The speed of sound is not a fixed number. Sound waves travel through air at around 760 miles per hour (343 meters per second) at sea level. Sound travels four times faster through water than it does through air, and around 13 times faster through steel. However, high in the atmosphere, where it is colder, the speed of sound decreases. Mach numbers compare the speed of an aircraft to the speed of sound where the plane is flying. So, Mach 2 is twice the speed of sound in air at a particular height.

TWO ITALIAN SCIENTISTS WERE THE FIRST TO CALCULATE THE SPEED OF SOUND IN THE 1660S.

Moving sounds

Sounds change as they move. If you stand still and watch an emergency vehicle zoom past with its siren blaring, the noise will be higher pitched as it approaches, and lower pitched as it drives away. This is known as the Doppler effect. The sound waves are emitted at the same frequency, but because the vehicle is getting closer, they take less time to reach you, and arrive at a higher frequency. It makes the siren sound different.

A train's blaring horn changes sound as it goes past.

THE DOPPLER EFFECT HAPPENS WITH SOUND, LIGHT, AND WATER WAVES.

Supersonic

If the vehicle is moving faster than the sound waves can move, we hear a different effect. In this case, the sound waves bunch together and create a high pressure zone. This leaves an area of low pressure right behind it, and makes a really loud noise called a sonic boom.

Melting moments

Let's not forget the gooey marshmallows. An object zooming through the air doesn't have a smooth passage. It is constantly bombarded by the air particles, which slow it down and produce heat. This is known as friction, or air resistance, and would (theoretically!) heat up the marshmallow enough to melt it, if it was moving fast enough.

A RAMP IS A MACHINE

If you want to push an object to a higher point, you'll need a ramp. A ramp is a type of simple machine and it can be combined with other machines to make compound machines.

Scientific work

Physicists examine forces and the effect they have on objects. A force is a push or a pull, and can happen at a distance or by making contact. Machines apply a force to an object; they do work. A ramp is a simple machine, and so are levers, wedges, pulleys, screws, and the wheel and axle.

Did You Know

Mountain animals look for natural ramps to climb upward more easily.

A PLAYGROUND SLIDE IS ALSO AN INCLINED PLANE.

Moving up

A ramp (properly called an inclined plane) is a flat surface with one end higher than the other. It allows an object to be moved higher, using less energy than lifting it straight up.

More machines

If you put two inclined planes back to back, you get another simple machine: a wedge. It is used to push objects apart. A knife, a chisel, and even your teeth are all wedges. A screw is a special kind of inclined plane. It is wrapped around a central pole and helps to lift things or hold them together. A lever is a really simple machine that is used all the time. It consists of a straight bar resting on a fulcrum (turning point) to multiply the force used.

Combined power

A bicycle is a fine example of a complex machine that uses many simple machines together. It has wheels and axles, pulleys (the chain on the gears), wedges (the gear teeth) and lots of levers and screws. Luckily, operating this complex machine is simpler than describing it!

The Egyptians used machines such as ramps for building the pyramids.

Did You Know

The pointed nose of a plane is a wedge, used for cutting through the air.

Move the levers around the fulcrum, and...snip!

Snip, snip!

Scissors are also a compound machine. The blades are a pair of wedges, attached to levers (the handles) which move around a fulcrum so they open and close.

A BATTERY AND BUNGEE JUMP BOTH STORE ENERGY

E nergy is all around us, in all sorts of forms. It is simply the ability to do work. It can be stored up, ready to use when it is needed. This is called potential energy.

On your marks...

Energy can be stored electrically in a battery, to put in your phone or remote control for when you want to use them. Objects can also have **potential energy** because of their position. If they are high up, they have the potential to be moved by **gravity**. A book resting on the edge of a table, a ball held in your hand, or a bungee jumper about to leap off the edge all have potential energy.

More energy

An object gains more potential energy as it moves higher. A heavy object has more potential energy than a light one.

THE ENERGY IN MOVING OBJECTS IS CALLED KINETIC ENERGY.

Get set...

An object can have potential energy if it is altered from its usual position. A spring at rest has no energy, but if you exert a force on it to squash it or stretch it, you transfer energy, which is stored until the spring is released again. The same happens when an archer draws back the string of a bow.

Go!

When an object starts moving, its potential energy is converted to **kinetic energy**. A sprinter at the starting line has potential energy until the gun goes off and he or she starts running. If you climb a mountain, your muscles pull against gravity to move your body upward. You draw on your supplies of chemical energy from your food. As you get higher, you gain potential energy. At the top, you can turn this stored energy back into kinetic energy by rappelling down.

Did You Know

Food contains chemical energy for living things to move, grow, and breed. It is often measured in joules or calories.

No pain, no gain

According to the laws of physics, energy can be converted from one form to another, but cannot be created or destroyed. The energy you use to climb the stairs is converted into potential energy by being higher up than you started.

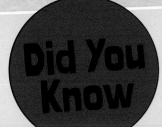

A KETTLE BOILS FASTER ON A MOUNTAINTOP

The higher you climb, the less air there is around you. The lower air pressure allows liquid to turn into gas more easily, so the boiling point of water is lowered. A kettle will boil more quickly.

THE REDUCTION IN AIR PRESSURE ALSO MAKES IT HARDER TO BREATHE AT HIGH ALTITUDES.

Climbing high

The gases in the air are constantly pressing down on us. If we are low down, at sea level, the whole of the atmosphere is on top of us, creating higher air pressure. As we climb higher, there is less air above us, and the pressure is reduced. It means that the water molecules inside a kettle need less heat energy to turn from liquid to gas and reach boiling point.

Under pressure

Pressure is the amount of force on a given area. A person wearing high heels is pressing with all their weight on a tiny space. Wearing snowshoes lowers the pressure, as a person's weight is spread across a much larger area. Pressure can be caused by many things. Water presses down, so there is higher pressure at the bottom of the ocean than on its surface. Deep-diving animals, such as sperm whales, have special lungs that can cope with being crushed.

Spreading your weight keeps you from sinking in the snow!

SCIENTISTS USE THE KELVIN SCALE TO MEASURE TEMPERATURE, RATHER THAN CELSIUS OR FAHRENHEIT.

A tight squeeze

How exactly does pressure affect temperature? Temperature is a measure of kinetic energy: how much the atoms are moving around. The atoms in cheese on a pizza have been given more energy by heating them. They are moving more freely, so the cheese melts and becomes runny. By lowering the air pressure, the atoms are less pressed together, so a smaller amount of heat is needed to free them from each other. It's like opening a jar of peanut butter: a loose lid requires less energy to take off than one that has been firmly screwed on.

Taking your temperature

Temperature can be measured with a thermometer. In many thermometers, a liquid is trapped in a glass tube. As the temperature increases, the liquid atoms move more and take up more space, so the reading on the thermometer goes up.

SNOW KEEPS YOU WARM

Snow is cold to touch, but if it is used to build a shelter against the cold air, it can stop the temperature from dropping. An igloo is much warmer inside than a tent.

In the air

Snow is made up of ice crystals that are packed together with a lot of air in between. Air is a poor conductor (carrier) of heat, and if it is trapped in one place, it prevents heat escaping. Heat travels from hot things to cold things, and moves through some substances better than others. Metals transfer heat quickly, so are good **conductors**. Gases (such as air), rubber, plastic, and wood do not allow heat energy through so easily. They are good **insulators**.

ANIMALS' FUR TRAPS AIR NEXT TO THEIR BODY TO KEEP THEM AT THE RIGHT TEMPERATURE.

Moving around

Heat can move around in three ways: conduction, **convection**, and **radiation**. Conduction happens when two things touch. If you hold a popsicle in your hand, the heat moves through the particles. Energy transfers from the fast-moving particles to the slower-moving ones, so your hand cools down and the popsicle heats up and melts. The bottom of a lava lamp contains a heater, which conducts heat energy to the glass and the wax inside.

Convection currents

Heat can travel through a liquid or a gas by convection. The hot, melted wax in a lava lamp becomes less dense and so it rises. It shares its heat as it does so, cooling and sinking back down again. At the bottom, it receives more heat, and rises. This also takes place in a pot of soup, a hot air balloon, and in the atmosphere, creating weather.

THE STUDY OF HEAT AND ENERGY IN PHYSICS IS CALLED THERMODYNAMICS.

Radiating rays

Conduction and convection need particles to transfer heat. Radiation carries heat on waves of light, usually infrared rays (see page 9). It can work through the vacuum of space, where there are no particles. The sun's warmth radiates through space to reach us here on Earth. Heat also radiates out from a campfire. A house radiator does not really radiate heat; it transfers it through the air by convection.

Radiated heat from the sun heats up Earth.

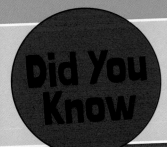

A BIRD ON A WIRE WON'T GET A SHOCK

Electricity wires are dangerous to people, but birds are quite safe... just as long as they don't touch anything else! That's because the birds are not giving the electricity a route to the ground.

Do not touch!

Electricity is the movement of **electrons**. These tiny particles will move from an area of "high electric potential" (where lots of electrons are packed) to an area of lower electric potential, where there is more room for them. Earth itself is so huge that it has a very low electric potential. If you touch a wire while also touching the ground, the electricity will flow through your body to reach the area with lowest electric potential.

Flowing electrons

A battery has a positive end, which has a high electrical potential, and a negative end, with lower electrical potential. When a battery is in use, it creates a circuit. The electrical charge moving through a circuit is called current. Current is measured in amperes (shortened to **amps**, or A) which tell you how fast it flows. A bulb may have 1 A of current, while a toaster uses about 9 A.

Breaking the loop

Electricity makes things work at the flick of a switch. How does that happen? No current flows when the switch is off, because the circuit is broken. In the on position, the switch completes the loop, and your lamp or TV or games console will work. A toy racing car has a metal contact which fits into a slot on the racetrack. When it touches the sides, electricity can flow.

I feel famous!

Power struggle

A battery supplies stored electricity for many toys and gadgets. The current flows from it in a single direction in a constant stream. It is called direct current, or DC. Household items that work from house current use alternating current, or AC. The famous scientist and inventor Thomas Edison was insistent that DC current was the way forward, but his rival Nikola Tesla (1856–1943) proved otherwise.

Thomas Edison
(1847–1931)

27

Did You Know

ELECTRICITY ZAPS BACK AND FORTH

If direct current (DC) flows in one direction, then alternating current (AC) constantly changes direction.

Back and forth

Electricity in your home is AC, not DC. When you plug in your TV, it connects to the electricity supply to give it power. The electrons in this circuit don't flow from point A to point B. Instead, they change direction 50 or 60 times per second, transferring electric current as they move. This cycle of changing directions is described as the frequency, and is measured in Hertz (just like sound waves; see page 14).

SOLAR CELLS CAN ONLY PRODUCE DC CURRENT. IT HAS TO BE CONVERTED INTO AC CURRENT TO BE USED IN THE HOME.

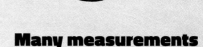
I'm certainly getting a shock!

Electricity flows like water, but don't mix the two of them!

Many measurements

Different properties of electricity are measured in different units. Hertz is the unit of frequency: how often it changes direction. Amps is the unit of current: how fast it is flowing. You will also hear **volts** and **ohms**. Imagine electricity is like water gushing out of a hose. As well as measuring how fast it flows you could also measure how much pressure is pushing it along; electrical pressure is measured in volts (V). A narrower hose will affect the flow, creating resistance, which is measured in ohms.

Making changes

Voltage, current, and resistance are linked. Altering one of them will affect the others. Imagine you turn up the pressure on your hose, or make the hose wider. More water will come out. Similarly, increasing the voltage or reducing the resistance will make more current flow.

Danger! High voltage!

Power plants send electricity over great distances. When electricity travels along cables, some energy is lost. If the current is reduced, so is the amount of lost energy. To reduce the current, the voltage is increased. High-voltage electricity travels extremely fast, but is very dangerous. Before it is delivered to our homes, it passes through a special transformer to reduce the voltage and make it safer (although it can still give you a nasty shock).

ELECTRICITY IS GENERATED AT 25,000 V, BUT SENT ALONG CABLES AT VOLTAGES UP TO 16 TIMES HIGHER.

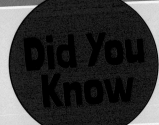
LIGHTNING STRIKES 100 TIMES EVERY SECOND

Lightning is a bright flash of electricity produced in a storm. It is very common: there are around 2,000 storms around the world at any time, most of them in the clouds.

Shocking!

Not all electricity flows in a current. Some is **static electricity**, which is electric charge that builds up in one place. It produces lightning, but on a smaller scale: it can cause the shock you feel when you wear certain shoes and then touch someone, or grab a metal door handle. It is caused by an imbalance between positive and negative electric charges.

Did You Know

Lightning is very powerful: it contains up to 1 billion volts and it is six times hotter than the surface of the sun.

30

Lightning strike

Frozen raindrops move around and bump into each other inside a storm cloud. The crashing around creates an electric charge, which is attracted to charges on the ground. Lightning zaps between the cloud and the ground to connect them. It is often called forked lightning because of the pattern it makes. Thunder occurs when the heat from lightning makes the air expand really quickly, causing vibrations.

In the air

Sometimes lightning stays within the clouds, as different charges at the highest points and lowest points are attracted to each other. Lightning in the air is often called sheet lightning. There are up to ten times as many flashes in the air as there are between clouds and the ground. Planes are often hit by lightning, but are protected so that the passengers do not get hurt.

AROUND 2,000 PEOPLE A YEAR ARE KILLED BY LIGHTNING STRIKES.

Getting to ground

Lightning tends to strike the highest thing in the area: a tree, an antenna, or a tall building. It can set them on fire and cause immense damage. In 1749, Benjamin Franklin, an inventor and politician, invented the lightning rod to protect buildings that may be struck. A tall metal pole on the roof is connected to a metal cable that leads to the ground. The metal conducts the electricity easily and quickly away from the building and into the earth.

The Empire State Building has a lightning rod as it is hit many times each year.

THE EARTH HAS TWO NORTH POLES

The Geographic North Pole is at the very top of Earth, and is the point Earth rotates around. The Magnetic North Pole can be nearby, but moves around all the time.

Mega magnet

Earth has a central core of molten iron that swirls and creates electric currents. This produces magnetic fields, and turns Earth into a giant magnet. Like all magnets, our planet has two opposite poles: north and south. The needle of a compass is attracted to Earth's magnetic north, not to its true geographic north. Changes under Earth's crust (top layer) make the magnetic north move on a daily basis.

AT THE NORTH POLE, THE SUN RISES IN MARCH AND SETS IN SEPTEMBER.

Which one, Ma?

An electromagnet can be switched on and off to move metals around.

On and off

Magnets come in different sizes, shapes, and forms. A bar magnet is a simple example. One end is north, the other end is south. It is surrounded by an invisible magnetic field which attracts some metallic objects (those containing iron, steel, nickel, or cobalt). Small items can be made temporarily magnetic by rubbing them along an existing magnet. An electromagnet is made by passing an electric current around an iron core. If it is switched off, the iron stops being magnetic.

Opposites attract

If you hold two magnets together, they will act in different ways. If opposite ends (N and S) are together, they will be attracted and stick to each other. If like ends (N and N or S and S) are together, they will repel. You will feel them trying to push each other away. A maglev train uses this principle to make it hover above the tracks without touching them.

Magnetic marvel

The sun belches out gases from its surface which make their way toward Earth. The magnetic field channels them to the poles where they bounce off oxygen and nitrogen atoms in the atmosphere, causing incredible light shows called the auroras.

A MAGNET STUCK TO YOUR REFRIGERATOR HAS MORE MAGNETIC FORCE THAN EARTH.

A BALL THROWN IN SPACE WILL NEVER STOP

If you throw a ball, it will keep going forever unless some sort of force acts upon it. On Earth, these forces include gravity and air resistance. Neither of those would really affect a ball thrown in space.

Down to Earth

All objects have their own gravity, pulling other things toward them. Generally it isn't strong enough to notice, but large objects (really large, like planets) have a gravitational pull that can affect other things. Earth's gravity is strong enough to keep you from floating off into space. If you throw a ball in the air, gravity brings it back down again. There are sections of space with nothing big enough to cause gravity.

THE MOON'S GRAVITY PULLS ON EARTH'S OCEANS, CAUSING THE TIDES.

It's the law

Gravity is a force, and acts on other objects to change them (see page 20). Scientists have three basic laws to describe motion and forces (thanks to Isaac Newton, who helped improve telescopes on page 7). It is the first of these laws that describes what happens with the ball in space. Namely, that any object in motion will continue to move in the same direction and speed unless forces act on it.

Large masses take larger forces to make them move.

A FORCE CAN MAKE AN OBJECT SPEED UP, SLOW DOWN, OR CHANGE DIRECTION.

Newton's second law...

...concerns forces, mass, and acceleration. Put simply, the more mass an object has, the more force it takes to make it move faster. It's obvious, really: it is harder to push a real car than a toy one. And if you exert more force, the car goes faster.

Number three

This law sounds complicated, but it really isn't. It states that for every action, there is an equal and opposite reaction. It simply means that when object A pushes on object B, object A gets pushed back in the opposite direction, equally hard. When you push back with your foot on the floor, it makes your skateboard move forward. When you sit on a chair, the chair (because of the materials and design) pushes back with an equal force, so it doesn't collapse and send you crashing to the ground.

Did You Know

SKIERS DON'T SKI ON SNOW

A ski presses down on compacted snow and melts a thin layer into water. The water reduces friction and allows the ski to slide over the surface more easily.

Slip sliding away

Friction occurs when two things slide together. It is a force that slows things down. Imagine pushing a heavy box across the floor. You would feel resistance, and that is friction. There is less friction between smooth things: the box would slide more freely across a wooden floor than on carpet. Skiers slide smoothly and quickly across the snow because the thin film of water puts up less resistance than the crunchy snow.

Did You Know

The dots on a basketball are called pebbles and are there to increase friction between your hand and the ball.

CROSS-COUNTRY SKIS ARE DESIGNED TO BOTH SLIDE AND GRIP ON THE SNOW.

Friction can explain why your hands hurt in the gym!

Getting hotter

Sliding things across each other can create heat. That is why you might rub your hands together in cold weather to warm them up. Friction slows things down, and the kinetic energy is transferred into heat energy. Without friction, you wouldn't be able to rub two sticks together to start a fire, or even strike a match. Friction can generate enough heat to burn your skin, such as holding a rope with your bare hands as you slide down.

Did You Know If it wasn't for friction, you would find it hard to stand, sit, or even lie in bed without sliding around.

The good...

Friction can be extremely useful, or it can cause problems. The brakes on a bicycle use friction to make it slow down and stop, by pressing a brake pad against the moving wheel. Friction between the ground and the wheels gives better grip on the road to make the bike move, and keep it from skidding.

... and the bad

However, friction between the moving parts of a vehicle wastes the energy being provided by the fuel. It can grind away the surface of the parts so they need replacing. Applying a **lubricant**, such as oil, will reduce the friction and make the engine run more efficiently and smoothly.

37

A PARACHUTE HAS A HOLE IN IT

A ir gathers underneath a parachute to act against gravity. A small hole is needed to help the parachutist stay in control instead of swinging dangerously in the sky.

A smooth descent

Air resistance is a type of friction, where a moving object pushes against the air. You can feel it on your face as you zoom down a hill on a bicycle or ride on a roller coaster. A person falling through the air is subject to gravity, pulling them to Earth. Using a parachute will slow their descent to make it safer. However, the air beneath the parachute ripples around as it tries to find a way out. The hole at the top allows the air to escape evenly, creating a smoother, safer ride.

I hope that hole is meant to be there!

AIR AND WATER RESISTANCE ARE SOMETIMES REFERRED TO AS DRAG.

A motorcyclist leans forward to increase the streamlining of the bike.

That's the point

Air is a combination of gases, all made up of molecules. A moving object has to push these molecules aside to be able to move through them. Some shapes, called streamlined shapes, move the molecules more effectively. The pointed nose of a plane is designed to help it fly efficiently. The world's fastest planes, cars, motorcycles, and even cyclists all use streamlining to reduce air resistance and increase their speed.

Falling down

Gravity pulls on all things equally. If you drop a brick and a feather from a tall building, gravity pulls them to Earth at the same rate. However, logic tells you that the brick would hit the ground first. That's because the feather is subject to more air resistance. Its surface fans out and hits more air, slowing it down.

Super swimmers

Water is also made up of molecules, and so creates resistance against moving objects. Competition divers and swimmers create a streamlined shape, with a small surface area, to cut through the water as neatly and efficiently as possible. Nature has many examples of superbly streamlined creatures, from sharks and penguins to dolphins and swordfish. Submarine designers have copied their shapes for their own use.

Did You Know

ASTRONAUTS DON'T SNORE

And they don't burp, either! It's all because their spacecraft is constantly falling and catching up with the pull of gravity. So it seems that there's no gravity on board.

Free passage

You snore because gravity pulls down your tongue and the soft tissue in your throat, so they partly block your windpipe Those soft bits vibrate (the snore) each time you breathe, just as a reed in a clarinet vibrates when air passes it. Except most people prefer the sound of a clarinet to a snore! Without gravity to pull those bits down, you don't wind up snoring.

ASTRONAUTS SOMETIMES GO ON A SPACEWALK TO CARRY OUT REPAIRS.

You can dream of becoming an astronaut; just don't expect to snore!

Testing, testing

Astronauts might be cooped up for months at a time, so it's important that they remain healthy. They're tested beforehand to make sure no problems become serious during a mission. It's also vital that they stay calm and are able to work with others. The bottom line? You'll fly high if you don't get on other people's nerves!

Bubble trouble

Anything that you let go on a spacecraft—peanuts, a crayon, or another astronaut in a sleeping bag—will float and drift around because there seems to be no gravity. Liquids gather in droplets because their molecules are drawn to each other. The outside is like an elastic layer which holds the molecules together in a sphere.

What a gas!

You don't have to worry about burping, either. That's also because of gravity, which is needed to separate gases from liquid in your stomach. Back on Earth, those gases bubble up from the stomach liquid and escape as burps. Without gravity, they stay mixed.

Did You Know Water doesn't flow in space.

ASTRONAUTS TRAIN IN SWIMMING POOLS TO GET USED TO MOVING AND WORKING IN EXTREME CONDITIONS.

Did You Know

NEPTUNE'S SUMMER LASTS 40 EARTH YEARS

Like Earth, Neptune has different seasons, with more sunlight in the summertime. However, as Neptune takes almost 165 years to go once around the sun, summer lasts for much, much longer.

Leaning over

Planets have seasons because their axis is slightly tilted. The axis is an invisible line through the middle, from top to bottom. Mercury spins neatly around an upright axis, but several other planets tilt, including Earth and Neptune. In summer, an area is tilted toward the sun. In winter, it is tilted away from the sun. On Earth, each hemisphere has four seasons. Places near the equator do not tip very much, so the weather stays the same all year round.

URANUS IS TILTED SO MUCH IT SPINS ON ITS SIDE, LIKE A BALL ROLLING ALONG THE GROUND!

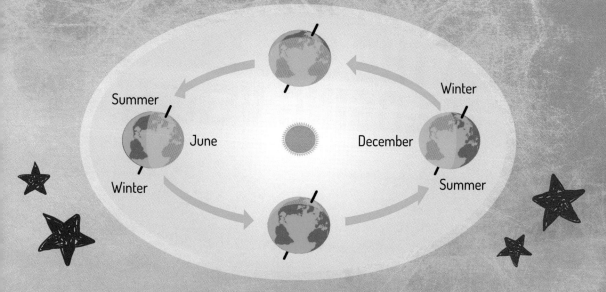

Summer

June

Winter

Winter

December

Summer

How seasons work

Imagine that each planet is an orange with a pin to show your country. If you hold the orange upright and walk it around a sun, the pin will always receive the same amount of light. Now tilt the orange slightly. On its next circuit, the pin will point more directly toward the sun for some of the time, and away from the sun for the rest of the time. The difference in the amount of sunlight creates different seasons.

A DAY ON VENUS LASTS FOR 243 EARTH DAYS WHILE A YEAR LASTS 225 EARTH DAYS.

In orbit

Astronomy, the study of stars, planets, and other items in space, is one of the oldest sciences. In the 1500s, a Polish astronomer, Nicolaus Copernicus, presented the theory that the planets orbit (circle) around the sun, and not around the Earth as was previously thought. It was controversial, but it led to many more discoveries about the solar system and the planets in it.

Day and night

At the same time as the planets orbit the sun, each one is rotating (spinning) on its own axis. The pin on your orange moves around, passing from day into night with each rotation. On Earth, this takes roughly 24 hours, but as every planet rotates at a different speed, the length of a day varies greatly. Jupiter has the shortest day of all: less than 10 Earth hours. Venus rotates so slowly that its day is longer than its year!

The sun sets every 24 hours on Earth.

THE SUN IS LOSING WEIGHT

Well, mass, scientifically speaking. The sun shines brightly because it is burning, using up energy. That energy comes from the fusion (joining together) of its main element, hydrogen, into helium.

Getting smaller...

The sun's interior consists of four separate areas with different things happening in each. At its heart is the core, the very hottest and densest part, made up of hydrogen atoms. At such high temperatures, and under such great pressure, these atoms join together to create helium. The helium atoms have less mass than hydrogen, and the difference in mass is released as light. Slowly but gradually, the sun is becoming less and less massive.

FUSION CAUSES THE SUN TO LOSE MORE THAN 4 MILLION TONS OF MASS EVERY SECOND!

...But bigger

The changes in the sun's core also affect its outer layers. Fusing hydrogen into helium reduces the number of particles and so the pressure decreases. To maintain balance, the outer layers expand ever so slightly, increasing the total distance across the sun. It's a tiny amount, with no effect on Earth's relation with the star we orbit around.

...And bigger

Eventually, the sun will get a LOT bigger, and turn into a **red giant**. The supply of hydrogen in the core will begin to run out and gravity will increase by such a huge amount that the sun will collapse into itself. The temperature will rise dramatically (and it's already superhot in there!) and the sun will swell in size and get brighter, turning it into a red giant. The planets closest to it will get burned up, and the outer planets' orbits will change. Earth will get swallowed up, or be too hot and dry to support life. Eventually the sun will collapse on itself to become a cooler **white dwarf**. It has enough fuel to burn for 5 to 7 billion years before this happens. though.

Don't panic, the sun won't burn out for billions of years!

Dying stars

Not all stars end their existence in the same way. It depends on their size. Stars bigger than our sun also collapse under their own gravity, but shrink rapidly enough to crush their own core, causing it to heat up so much it explodes in a **supernova**. Their remains may turn into a **black hole**, where gravity is so strong that not even light can escape. They have enormous mass; a black hole of just one atom can have the mass of a mountain!

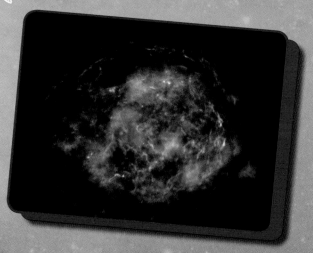

Glossary

amp (short for ampere) The unit of measurement for the rate at which an electric current is flowing.

amplitude The distance between the middle or rest position and the highest or lowest point of a wave.

black hole A place in space where gravity is so strong that not even light can escape.

conductor A material that electricity or heat can flow through easily.

convection The way that heat is transferred from one place to another through a liquid or a gas.

decibels (dB) A measure of the loudness of a sound.

electron One of the tiny (subatomic) particles that make up atoms with a negative electrical charge.

frequency The number of waves per second in a sound wave.

friction The resistance between two surfaces when they rub together.

fusion Joining two things together.

gravity A force that tries to pull two objects towards each other.

hertz (Hz) The measurement of the frequency of a sound wave, measured by the number of cycles (complete up and down movements of the wave) per second.

incandescence The light that is produced by heat.

insulator A material that allows little or no electricity or heat to flow through it.

kinetic energy The energy of moving objects.

lubricant A substance such as oil or grease that is used to reduce friction between two surfaces.

luminescence Cold light not produced from heat.

mass The amount of matter in an object.

molecule A group of atoms bonded together.

ohm The unit of measurement of resistance to current in an electrical circuit.

potential energy The stored energy in an object.

prism A triangular glass block that refracts light as it passes through.

radiation Energy that is transferred as waves or moving particles.

red giant A very large star.

refract To bend light as it passes through a different material (such as water).

spectrum The band of colors that make up white light.

static electricity An electric charge produced by an imbalance of positive and negative charges.

supernova The explosion of a star.

supersonic Faster than the speed of sound.

ultrasound A high-frequency sound – so high that humans cannot hear it.

ultraviolet (UV) Invisible rays that are part of the energy that comes from the sun.

vacuum An empty space in which there is no air or any other matter.

volt (V) The unit of measurement for how strongly an electrical current is flowing around a circuit.

white dwarf A small, very dense star.

Further Information: Websites

www.physics.org
A comprehensive guide to physics on the web, with fun facts, experiments, and links to checked sites for a wide range of physics topics.

www.physicscentral.com
American Physical Society website invites you to "learn how your world works."

www.physics4kids.com/index.html
A good overview of basic physics information about motion, electricity and magnetism, and light and optics, with fun quizzes on each topic.

www.sciencekids.co.nz/physics.html
A fun website with physics facts, quizzes, games, experiments, videos, and images.

www.solarsystemscope.com
Interactive website that allows you to go deep into our solar system.

Publisher's note to educators and parents: Our editors have carefully reviewed these websites to ensure that they are suitable for students. Many websites change frequently, however, and we cannot guarantee that a site's future contents will continue to meet our high standards of quality and educational value. Be advised that students should be closely supervised whenever they access the Internet.

Further Information: Books

Big Questions: Can You Feel the Force? by Richard Hammond (Dorling Kindersley, 2010)

Light and Dark by Daniel Nunn (Raintree, 2012)

Light and Sound by Richard and Louise A. Spilsbury (Heinemann Educational, 2013)

Physics: Investigate the Forces of Nature by Jane P. Gardner (Nomad Press, 2014)

Super Science: Light and Sound Experiments by Chris Oxlade (Miles Kelly, 2011)

Index